TO TOUCH HEAVEN

*Dear Fr. Tamiro,
You were the inspiration for me to write this!
Blessings forever
Patty B.*

TO TOUCH HEAVEN

Where the Invisible Becomes Visible

PATRICIA MARIE BLUEMEL

iUniverse, Inc.
Bloomington

To Touch Heaven
Where the Invisible Becomes Visible

Copyright © 2011 by Patricia Marie Bluemel

All rights reserved. No part of this book may be used or reproduced by any means, graphic, electronic, or mechanical, including photocopying, recording, taping or by any information storage retrieval system without the written permission of the publisher except in the case of brief quotations embodied in critical articles and reviews.

This is a work of fiction. All of the characters, names, incidents, organizations, and dialogue in this novel are either the products of the author's imagination or are used fictitiously.

iUniverse books may be ordered through booksellers or by contacting:

iUniverse
1663 Liberty Drive
Bloomington, IN 47403
www.iuniverse.com
1-800-Authors (1-800-288-4677)

Because of the dynamic nature of the Internet, any web addresses or links contained in this book may have changed since publication and may no longer be valid. The views expressed in this work are solely those of the author and do not necessarily reflect the views of the publisher, and the publisher hereby disclaims any responsibility for them.

Any people depicted in stock imagery provided by Thinkstock are models, and such images are being used for illustrative purposes only.

Certain stock imagery © Thinkstock.

ISBN: 978-1-4502-8970-2 (sc)
ISBN: 978-1-4502-8971-9 (dj)
ISBN: 978-1-4502-8972-6 (ebk)

Library of Congress Control Number: 2011900970

Printed in the United States of America

iUniverse rev. date: 01/25/2011

To

Joanna y Luis

Contents

Acknowledgments xi
Preface xiii
Introduction xv

Part 1: The I Am Not

The I Am Not. 3
The Pier Top 4
The Wake-Up Call 6
How Did I Get Here? 7
Graduation 9
Beginning the Quest 10
The Lure of the Divine Proportion 12
The Meeting of Father K. 13

Part 2: The He Did

The He Did	19
The Pilgrimage	20
The Lalibela Moment	22
An Introduction to a Hidden Mystery	24
Lalibela, a New Jerusalem	28
The Creations	31
Father K.'s Special Retreat	32
An Interlude	36
The Precious Human Body	37
The Anointing	40
The Blessing	42
The Manuscript	44

Part 3: The I Am

The I Am	49
Returning Home	50
Reintegrating	53
One Morning in Chemistry Class	54
A Distant Memory	55
St. Joseph Parish	57
Father Thomas	59
The Worst Part of It	61
The End Result	63
The Real Facts	64
When People Are Used	66
A Hidden Wisdom	68
A Miracle Priest	71
The Chalice of the Silver Maple	73
Resurrection of the Manuscript	76
Rereading the Manuscript	78
The Next Day	82
The Mystical Bailey Roe	84
The Miracle	86
You Knew This Would Happen	89
A Final Reflection	91

Part 4: Living in the I Am

A Time for Celebration 95
The Nature of the Pilgrim 97
Medjugorje 99
Reentry Back into the World 101
Teaching *To Touch Heaven* 103

Acknowledgments

The writing of this book is a result of the extraordinary encouragement, support, and companionship of dear friends.

I am especially grateful to the morning coffee clan, Peggy Bushwaller and Louise Brush, who listened and offered every support during the Silver Maple crisis.

I can never repay Sharon Kenny for her healing touch contributing to my well-being, Elaine Regal for her consultations on the nature of truth, Ellen Bachman for her inspiration, Sister Paul and Sister Grace for always being there, Renate Thevarajah for our international discussions, and Maureen Ryan for her faithful support for so many years.

I am eternally grateful to my godmother, Lena Blansfield, who kept me in the faith during every challenge.

To Joan Skedd, I cannot say enough words of appreciation for always seeing the miracle that I could not see ahead of me.

I especially thank Penny Pohlman for her unbelievable generosity, without which I would not have had the resources to continue my work.

Our lives are a spiritual journey through the

I Am Not,

the

He Did,

and

the

I Am.

—Patricia Marie Bluemel

Preface

Dear Fellow Pilgrim,

To Touch Heaven is neither a traditional novel nor a memoir. It is probably best described as a spiritual narrative, a contemplation, and a reflection on life's spiritual pilgrimage—its three distinct phases.

Though *To Touch Heaven* is based on a true story, all of the characters are to be regarded as representing a "corporate" concept.

Katherine, the main character, represents *all* pilgrims on their respective journeys. Sister Paul Emilia represents not only the Dominican charism but also angels sent to pilgrims on their journeys. The priests represent not only pastors but also those spiritual directors who come along to guide us to the next stage of awareness. The cathedrals of Lalibela represent not only spectacular examples of exotic architecture, but also that place where our souls find a home while on earth. The Stillbornes—as a couple—represent our present society, the corporate personality of our nation in 2011. No one character reflects in any way any *real* person.

The details, appearances, and mannerisms of the characters are intentionally left to the imagination of the reader so as not to detract from the main purpose of the book—the three phases of the spiritual journey.

The main conflict of the story may be unclear to the casual reader. One must follow the pilgrim through each phase—the I Am Not, the He Did, and the I Am. This is a story not of the physical domain or of a psychological drama as can be found in a traditional novel, but rather a story of the *journey of the soul.*

The reader must rely on his or her imagination to fill in details that are not explicit. The reader may find that not much detail is given regarding certain decisions the main character makes—for example, why she leaves paradise to follow her husband to Ethiopia. However, this would detract from the main purpose of the text; it would return the story to a psychological drama, whereas the sole purpose of this work is to articulate the basic phases of the journey of a pilgrim's soul.

The intention of the book is to bring the reader to a point where he or she questions his or her own life pilgrimage and own passage through the I Am Not, the He Did, and the I Am, which then offers the further possibility of discernment of one's life calling, life vocation, and purpose in life.

Blessings,
Patricia Marie Bluemel, director
The To Touch Heaven programs

Introduction

The I Am Not

In the beginning, the earthly pilgrim is held hostage

by a strange compass, that ever-present companion,

an ever-present void *governing the human heart.*

If the earthly pilgrim does not keep vigilant,

if the pilgrim does not keep wide awake,

the heart is easily seduced, easily enticed, easily

drawn in every direction—sometimes to very strange

and forbidden shores—all in an effort, that continuous quest, to fill that deep chasm of emptiness, *to fill that*

ever-present void, *leaving the pilgrim full*

of longing.

The He Did

It is at this point that God, in his great mercy,

seems to erupt *into our* void, *filling it*

miraculously with an eternal joy!

The Word now has acquired an ear, *and it becomes*

the eternal foundation—the filling of the soul with

an elixir of pure delight.

The new ears *that can now* hear *wait in great anticipation for the next* divine eruption.

Advancing in spirituality, the pilgrim is conditioned to

this new sensitivity, to the delicate hiddenness

of the divine source and is given new eyes *for*

this higher attainment of discerning the mystery.

The I Am

A vision of the divine eruption manifests, and the pilgrim miraculously is able **to touch heaven.**

Part 1

The I Am Not

The I Am Not

Dear Pilgrim, all of the angels and saints are

praying for you.

They pray that you may find the true source of all joy!

All of heaven holds its breath as you look here and

there to find this priceless knowledge.

Oh, Pilgrim, if you just knew how all of creation

holds its breath in hope for your successful journey.

The Pier Top

It was an evening of pinks and purples. We were at the Pier Top Lounge, perched high above paradise.

There, in the light of a setting fireball sun, our waiter popped a champagne cork. Bubbles of delight filled our glasses, and the city seemed to melt into a thousand and one diamond-like lights.

"Life is so good," I thought. "We are here in this paradise—exquisite yachts in every direction, multimillion-dollar condos along the beach, mansions glimmering near the waterway, and then those cruise liners, those bastions of fantasy illuminating the harbor …"

"What more could there be?" I suggested to my husband.

We toasted once again, and then JB leaned forward, rested his glass firmly on the table, smiled, and became more serious. "Let's leave all this—the million-dollar view, this paradise! Let us sell everything we have and go to Africa and really live our lives."

I responded with a nervous laugh.

JB just smiled.

"You are serious!"

"Yes, I am."

I went silent. I knew at that very moment that my life had drastically changed forever!

The Wake-Up Call

My wake-up call was a blood-curdling cry from the nearby mosque, the early-morning call to prayer, reminding me that I was not at home but rather in Africa ... Ethiopia ... Addis Ababa.

The first day started with cold showers, cultural indoctrinations, drinking Ethiopian coffee—not with sugar or cream but salt and rancid butter.

Everything here felt strange, foreign. The food, the language, even the alphabet—are not our western letters but rather Ethiopian letters called fidels—and most of all, their concept of time.

In Ethiopia, the day begins at 6:00 a.m., not 12:00 a.m., there is a thirteen-month calendar, and the calendar itself is eight years behind our own, so that it is not 2010 here, but rather 2002.

All of this on the first morning here, and it was only noon. What could possibly be next?

How Did I Get Here?

The next thing was a ride through the city of Addis Ababa.

Our driver wove in and out of traffic, yielding right and then turning sharply left, dodging donkeys overloaded with all sorts of goods and black-fuming buses crammed with humanity.

With an abrupt swerve and stop, our driver and instructor invited us for coffee. It was a lesson, of course, in how to negotiate such a city. In nanoseconds, our truck was surrounded by a crowd of children crying for money and knocking on the windows. "Money for us! Money for us!"

JB opened my door, grabbed my hand, and pulled me through the crowd as a boy on all fours with wooden blocks strapped to his knees pulled on my skirt with his mouth.

Inside, we were quiet, recovering from the imposing crowd. The instructor lectured on how one must be quick—no time to pause—and be aggressive in moving through the crowds.

The "bunabet," a coffee shop, was plain—no frills, no décor, with empty shelves and unclean tables. Somehow, I knew deep down that this was *the introduction* to my new life.

JB, untouched by the meager surroundings, engaged in lively conversation with the instructor while I sat and wondered, "Just how did I get here—here at this coffee shop? Shouldn't I be in Paris at an elegant bistro?"

Graduation

How did I get to be at that coffee shop? It started at high school graduation, that day of high excitement and high anticipation.

The keynote speaker was a woman. Her name is long erased from my aging memory bank, but she managed to redirect my life.

Entering the graduation hall, I was sure that *happiness* was what I wanted out of life.

Midway during the ceremony, during the keynote address, I became ambivalent. The speaker suggested, "Do not settle for anything less in life than *to touch heaven.*"

Somehow, this notion—this idea of devoting one's life *to touching heaven*—overcame me. I found myself transported into new heights of inspiration.

And so, from that very moment, *to touch heaven* became my life.

Beginning the Quest

I grew up in paradise—a garden of aquamarine waters, white-powdered beaches, swaying palms. My childhood was spent on a dreamy sixty-foot, gaff-rigged schooner decked with golden trailboards, ratlines, and a fifteen-foot bowsprit. The *Island Trader* was the pirate ship of its day, noticed wherever she went, sparking conversation and intrigue.

I spent my early adult life lying in the net of the bowsprit, reading and playing with the dolphins as they swam alongside. It was here that the beauty of creation captivated me, and so I made the logical conclusion that *to touch heaven* required me to make a study of it.

So I studied biology at the University of Miami, a pathway demanding innumerable dissections and memorization of anatomical charts.

"To understand biology in more depth," one professor recommended, "you should study chemistry."

And so I embarked on a long journey of foul-smelling chemistry labs and memorization of chemical formulas, learning the art of balancing equations and calculating moles.

After that, a chemistry professor suggested that, to really understand chemistry in depth, I should make a study of physics. So I found myself struggling with the basics of movement, everything in the cosmos being reduced to math.

I received my bachelor of science and realized that I had not yet managed *to touch heaven*, so graduate school must be the next logical step.

At Bucknell University, I studied cellular biology and statistics, and I spent most of my time in the laboratory.

At graduation for a master of science, I realized that I had not yet *touched heaven*. I clutched my diploma and wondered, "What is next?"

The Lure of the Divine Proportion

A letter was what came next—from the US Army—offering a direct commission as a first lieutenant. Desperate for science-trained personnel—linguists—the letter outlined an exciting career as a cryptologist.

The study of codes and symbols led to glyphs and ultimately to the divine proportion. It had a special seduction—the golden mean, the sacred cut, the revelation of numbers, the secret of simple patterns of numbers found not only in simple mathematics but also in music and throughout nature and science. It was alluring, and I dedicated hours of my free time to exploring it. I was consumed with the pursuit of understanding.

The more I read, and the more I became involved with popular notions of truth, the more muddled life seemed to become. Instead of nearing heaven, I felt that it was more elusive than ever.

And then JB came into my life—a handsome, well-traveled doctor, a physician committed to helping the less fortunate. He convinced me to marry him and to start a new path in service to others—and that this might be a better path in search of heaven.

The Meeting of Father K.

Fast-forward now from graduate school, the US Army, and my marriage to JB to Ethiopia and the meeting of Kes Kafalyew, better known to the English speaking as Father K., an Ethiopian priest—trained Jesuit—with an Irish accent.

We were in the backseat of an old Land Rover on an arduous journey from Gambala to Addis Ababa, a ride over dusty roads, up steep inclines, and through rough, mountainous terrain.

This long trip afforded one thing, and that was plenty of time for me to share my now rather long story—my quest *to touch heaven*.

My tale was further complicated by the events of living within a mission, the sometimes bizarre behavior of missionaries, the challenges of different nationalities, and other exotic incidents of outback life.

"I am no longer sure that the Christian life is a real possibility, something attainable," I explained. "And so I have resigned myself to an alternative spiritual pathway, especially after living with missionaries."

Father K. smiled. For a moment, he scanned the mountainous landscape, and then, with his green eyes, he looked directly into my soul. "You need to be taken away from books—and, I guess, missionaries." He returned his gaze to the landscape.

There was a long pause in our conversation, as though he was remembering something profound.

"When creation is reduced to mathematical equations, when it has lost a respect for the deep mystery, awe and wonderment are lost. Science in this form is lethal, and in a way, it is suicidal. Reductionist science is simply *improper knowledge*. This is what you are suffering from—*improper knowledge*, improper education. Trust me, I know. I have been there … twelve years at Cambridge." He smiled. "This is now the great root of suffering of mankind, reducing life to technology, math, and equations. It is a relativism of all truth. The result is that humanity is lost. Remember one thing—we need *being* for truth, we need the *human body* to understand and perceive truth, and we require a body to have a sense of awe and mystery. This is why life is so *precious,* and that is what should be the constant crusade of the church."

"And so?" I responded.

"What you need is *proper knowledge*—what we call Eternal Wisdom—and then you will *touch heaven*," he answered. "You need the experience of God in addition to that of books and science and missionaries. This new knowledge, this proper knowledge, is your answer. It embraces something beyond the mathematical equation. It accepts the everlasting mystery of things, and it helps us to even accept the missionary and his shortcomings."

"And so what graduate school provides this *proper knowledge*?" I inquired.

"It is not found in a graduate school or university. It can be found, however, in a *hidden holy land* not known yet throughout the world. It is truly a special place. It is called Lalibela."

"Lalibela? Where might that be?"

"It is here—here in Ethiopia!"

My eyes widened in amazement. And by hearing the word *Lalibela*, I sensed that something big was about to happen in my life. Though I could not articulate it at the time, the I Am Not phase of my life had come to a close.

Part 2

The He Did

The He Did

Dear Pilgrim, all of the angels and saints and now

all of creation is celebrating, because your

He Did encounter is near!

The heavens are lighted, and the choirs of angels are

singing!

For today, all heaven and earth smile,

and there is joy

everywhere!

The Pilgrimage

Father K. had secretly arranged everything, which inspired a whirlwind of activity—a rush to submit forms and documents, the request to the Ethiopian government for permission to travel to an unauthorized site, the chartering of a bush plane, the packing of food, water, and sleeping bag—and then there I was, suddenly at the airport in safari pants, a hat, hiking boots, and two backpacks.

The inner cabin shook, and the propellers swirled. Two monks, a priest, a passenger from the French embassy, and I buckled up, and the plane began to roar as we taxied the potholed runway of the airport in Addis Ababa.

In minutes, the sprawl of Addis Ababa gave way to the countryside and the familiar grass huts and endless land. We ascended up into the gem-rich mountains of northern Ethiopia, sparkling at once in emerald and then ruby with sprinkles of sapphire and gold.

And so I was off, on my way to find *Eternal Wisdom*—the proper knowledge, as Father K. put it—to see the Face of Christ.

Two hours later, the pilot politely interrupted our quiet meditations, explaining the flight plan and the mountaintop landing to take place shortly after flying over the next ridge.

The bush plane soared up and then zoomed down—straight down—the engines stuttering, the pilots speaking loudly in Amharic, turning to the passengers with gestures of reassurance.

The monks remained calm and centered in their contemplations. My eyes were squeezed shut as we touched down and came to a quick halt on the runway, which was a level area of rock on the mountaintop.

The bush plane had stopped by the one and only tree where an Ethiopian and a minibus were waiting for us, the arrivals.

As I scanned the scenery, I wondered, "Where is the Eternal Wisdom and the face of Christ?" It was not on the rusted bus grinding its way down and then up the steep inclines, winding its way to Lalibela. We pulled into the Seven Olives Hotel and were informed promptly that there was no water till 6:00 p.m. and only two items on the dinner menu.

The Lalibela Moment

My guide, also a monk, greeted me at the hotel.

"Father K. has told me all about you," he said, grinning.

"Oh, dear," I responded.

"It is time for you to come with me. We are going to climb a mountain. Come follow me now." He smiled.

It was no easy feat. Exhaustion took over, but the guide, Brother Benedict, kept urging me to the top, assuring me of a great revelation.

As I reached the crest at the top, Brother Benedict grabbed my arm, slowed me down, and held me steady. As I looked down, my eyes widened with amazement, my heart beat wildly, and my mind stopped. Paralyzed, I was struck silent. I could not utter one word!

The air was suddenly perfumed, filled with divine suggestion, a thousand and one partial apprehensions of another world. I remember what seemed to be a chorus of angels, a flutter of feathers, and the sound of a door creaking open, revealing an incredible *light*. And in that instant, that nanosecond, *I touched heaven*.

Hundreds of feet below me was St. George's Cathedral, sculpted out of the earth and hewn in the top of the mountain with architectural perfection. Hundreds of chanting priests surrounded it.

There was a profusion of *light*. In every direction, it was luminous and radiant, exquisite in every way, and there was an infinite power of *presence* exuding a pure *joy* and a sense of the miraculous. It seemed like a silent rejoicing, and then Brother Benedict whispered to me, "You have just experienced the *Lalibela Moment*, the *Lalibela Blessing*, Eternal Wisdom, the Face of Christ."

An Introduction to a Hidden Mystery

The steps were steep down to the base of the cathedral. "Think of this descent as an entry into the womb of our Blessed Mother," Brother Benedict said with a smile. He looked at me and sighed. "I can sense you do not know her."

"No, that part of Christianity is foreign to me."

"Think of her this way, then. Mary is the one who teaches humanity the *purpose* of their human bodies. She teaches us about pregnancy and about giving everything to *Christ*."

"Wow," I interjected. "I have taught the biology of the human body for years, and I have never heard this before."

"Well, then, since I have piqued your interest, let me continue," Brother Benedict said with a grin. "Mary is that creature who was able to be pregnant with *Christ*; she was able to birth *him*. She is actually a model for all Christians. *We* are *all* to become pregnant with *Christ*. What do you think of that?"

Brother Benedict paused, taking a rest on the steps of the cathedral before he continued, "You could say that *pregnancy* is the true state of the *Christian pilgrim*. To be pregnant with Christ is what we are called to be—to give birth to *him* in every task we do, every encounter we have, in every challenge we face."

"This is really amazing!"

He paused again as the priests in procession with huge crosses began to bless the pilgrims who had journeyed to Lalibela on foot.

"When you come to know Mary, you will encounter the fullness of *Christ*. This path of Mary to Christ is for *everyone*. She has been a carefully *hidden* secret until this time on the planet, and now she is sent to unify us all and to point to her *son*. Father K. shared with me that so far in your life, you have used books and science to find *truth*, and that is admirable, but Mary is the fastest way to encounter it."

The sun was setting. One of the priests with a huge gold cross approached us, chanted, and blessed us both.

Brother Benedict smiled, took my hand, and continued, "Lalibela is like a Mary. It is hidden like Mary. One cannot see Lalibela from any place but standing at the edge of a chasm. She is the womb that carried Christ, and Lalibela is like a huge womb. Pilgrims come down into the earth, into the silence, and they enjoy the sense of protection, silence, and peace. As they ascend the stairs, they meditate on their birth by *Mary* into *Christ*."

We walked past three other cathedrals, one more awesome than the other.

"Lalibela is a school of Mary. Here, one learns about her and takes her on as a life model for *true spiritual pregnancy*. Do not miss the opportunity in the few days you are here to be introduced to the greatest pathway to Christ—that of Jesus living in Mary."

We left the steps of the cathedral to follow the procession.

"So why has this not been taught? I've never heard anything like this. Mary was a statue taken out at Christmastime; she appeared on Christmas cards and then was gone by New Year's," I shared.

Brother Benedict laughed. "Well, that is true of most Christians, but what theologians are sensing is that Mary's second mission is now starting. She is to usher in a Second Advent. You will probably hear more about her in the coming years. For sure, there are more and more apparitions, more calling on her help, more seeking a closer relationship with her.

"The incredible aspect of Mary is that she is honored by all of the major religions—Judaism, because she was a Jewish maiden, Islam, who honors her as the mother of a great prophet, and of course Christianity, where she is honored as the Mother of our Lord.

"Her beauty alone is so attractive to us, her gentleness is so enticing, and her grace is so healing. Humanity needs that, especially now, more than ever, and her only mission is to prepare the way for the pilgrim to know her *son*.

"So, this evening, ask Mary to come to you and take your hand to show you her son, *Christ*—or, as your Father K. would say, *proper knowledge*."

Lalibela, a New Jerusalem

The bells of the cathedral announced *Lauds*, the liturgical time of the first light. The pilgrims were already on foot back to the cathedrals for morning devotions.

"Good morning. I hope you slept well," Brother Benedict said. "Let us go now before we are late."

There was a crescendo of music. The priests began their chants, and the scent of incense was again everywhere.

"Today," offered Brother Benedict, "sense that this pilgrimage is one from the profane to the sacred, that you are now truly in *another world*. Let the morning devotion slow your mind and take you to a place of peace, and afterward, we will take a nice walking tour."

After the service, Brother Benedict and I began our walk. "Lalibela is the *New Jerusalem*. This place has been designed as an exact replica of the old Jerusalem. There is a River Jordan here, a Garden of Olives, and a Golgotha. But what is so profound here, what makes Lalibela so amazing, is that it was once home to the Ark of the Covenant. Hence, the twelve cathedrals here are all interconnected by a sophisticated labyrinth of interconnecting tunnels that are just big enough to move the Ark from one cathedral to another for safekeeping."

"Is it by chance still here?" I inquired.

Brother Benedict grinned. "The Ark, considered to be the most priceless religious relic, suggests the Temple of Jerusalem as the place where God dwells with his people."

I felt an indescribable energy, a *lightness*, a peace, and *joy*! What this had to do with Ark, I did not yet understand.

"Mary is the hinge between the Old and New Testament. She is the new Ark. The old Ark, the Ark of the Covenant, was the receptacle for the Law written in stone. Mary is the New Ark, the receptacle of the Law, now the Word enfleshed as *the Christ*." Brother Benedict continued his instruction as we slowly walked on. "That is why Lalibela is a place of miracles and healings. Thousands upon thousands of pilgrims have come here asking Mary to show them the Face of Christ."

We stepped aside, leaving the crowd of pilgrims, and Brother Benedict explained, "Many come here to die, to be in a holy place, to be as close to heaven on earth as possible before crossing over."

We passed by Golgotha. There, hundreds upon hundreds of skulls and bones were clearly visible, a potent reminder to the pilgrim of what life is really about—an invitation for reflection.

The sun began to set. The priests still chanted, new pilgrims waited for their special blessings, incense continued to fill the air, and I felt transported as to the edge of heaven.

"If you leave here without understanding what this place is, you say, 'I have been to Lalibela,' but if you leave here understanding what this place is, you have been a successful pilgrim, and you say, 'I have been to *Lalibella*.'"

The Creations

It was an evening gathering of pilgrims. We sat on the ground outside one of the cathedrals. Father K. had arrived from Addis Ababa by Land Rover, and he was to be the retreat master. His subject was *the creations*.

"Welcome, brothers and sisters in Christ. Welcome, dear pilgrims, Ethiopians and foreigners alike. Welcome! This evening, I share with you one wisdom which is helpful for you in enhancing your experience of Lalibela. As you should know—" Father K. paused and smiled, and the pilgrims then laughed. "God fashioned the physical creation in seven days—technically six days, and then he rested. But that is *physical creation*—the sea, the flowers, the mountains, the rabbits, and so on. But few Christians are aware that there was also a *spiritual creation*. It, too, took seven days. By the spiritual creation, we are talking about the Tabernacle of Moses. God revealed the precise measurements and construction of this Tabernacle. God had the Tabernacle built *because* this is where he said he would come to *dwell* with his people, with his creation. The incredible aspect of the Tabernacle is that it is the place where *the invisible becomes visible*. This should make us all silent for a couple of hours. We can summarize, then, that God enjoys a home—a dwelling place to be with his people—and for some reason, he required this kind of design, this kind of home here on earth, so that *he* can become present."

Father K.'s Special Retreat

"So what is this special design, this sacred design, which God requests to have on earth so *he* can come among us? It is indeed one of the greater mysteries of our Christian faith. The Tabernacle is in some way a cryptogram—that is, a cipher, a code. Sometimes, it occurs to me that God really enjoys math and encoded messages." He laughed. "I will attempt to open up this mystery for you tonight in the simplest way I can. It will be impossible to share with you every last detail. That which you do not receive tonight, you can take on as a study for the rest of your life." He chuckled. "Are you ready?"

The pilgrims applauded.

"Lalibela reveals the nature of the sacred design, the design of the Tabernacle, that construction that God revealed to us as the architecture for *his house* on earth. See the book of Exodus for all of the details.

"Lalibela is special, because it hints of the Ark of the Covenant, which was the most special object in the Tabernacle. The Ark of the Covenant prefigures Mary, the Blessed Mother, who is referred to as the Second Ark.

"The Tabernacle is an elaborate design. Everything about this Tabernacle teaches us about how to meet God, how to encourage *his presence* among us. To understand the Tabernacle of Moses is to enter a far deeper mystery of God. It is a sacred design that not only applies to the Tabernacle itself, but was used later to design the Temple of Solomon and the Temple in Jerusalem. And we see it in the design of our cathedrals, our church. Inside such a design, we actually are able *to touch heaven*, so powerful is this use of this sacred design.

"Now here you are sitting in Lalibela with twelve such cathedrals, twelve such sacred designs in one small place. It explains some of the incredible peace and energy we feel here.

"Stay with me; I know it is getting late, but the Tabernacle of Moses—which housed the Ark of the Covenant where God came in the form of a cloud—is also the sacred design for the New Ark. We know this New Ark to be Mary, who was the home for the living God made flesh—the Christ.

"Listen *now*; this is the amazing *secret*. The Tabernacle of Moses is also the sacred design of the *precious human body*. It is the design partly of the physical human body, but more so the design of the *spiritual human body*—the new biology, the new creation! The Tabernacle suggests a biotheology of the new creation."

There was a hush and then gasps of realization and amazement as Father K. made a long pause.

"One can spend a lifetime studying this most amazing cryptogram of life. Every aspect of it reveals the *precious design of the human body*. I can provide a brief preview of what the Tabernacle design reveals.

"The outer court represents unconscious man, the lower half of the human body. The inner court—conscious man—is the upper half of the human body. The brazen altar, upon which a pilgrim must make a sacrifice in order to enter the inner court, represents the digestive system of the human body. The laver, that place in which the pilgrim purifies him or herself before entering the inner court, also represents the kidneys of the human body. The candelabra is a symbol of wisdom, the brain, and so forth. This just touches the surface.

"Those who leave here and align their lives with this sacred design, with Mary as the model of perfection of the sacred design, make themselves a *true dwelling place* for the Lord. Use the sacred design in your homes and offices, and use the sacred design to plan your day. If you do so, I promise that you will feel the *anointing* that you have been promised. For if the pilgrim is true and manages to arrive at the door of the Holy of Holies and then enter, that pilgrim is promised the *anointing,* the blessing, the miracle. Do not forget it. Do not stop until you are there in the *sancta sanctorum*.

"This evening, contemplate the notion that Mary is the *spiritual creation* giving life to *the Christ*.

"It is late now, so I wish you a blessed evening."

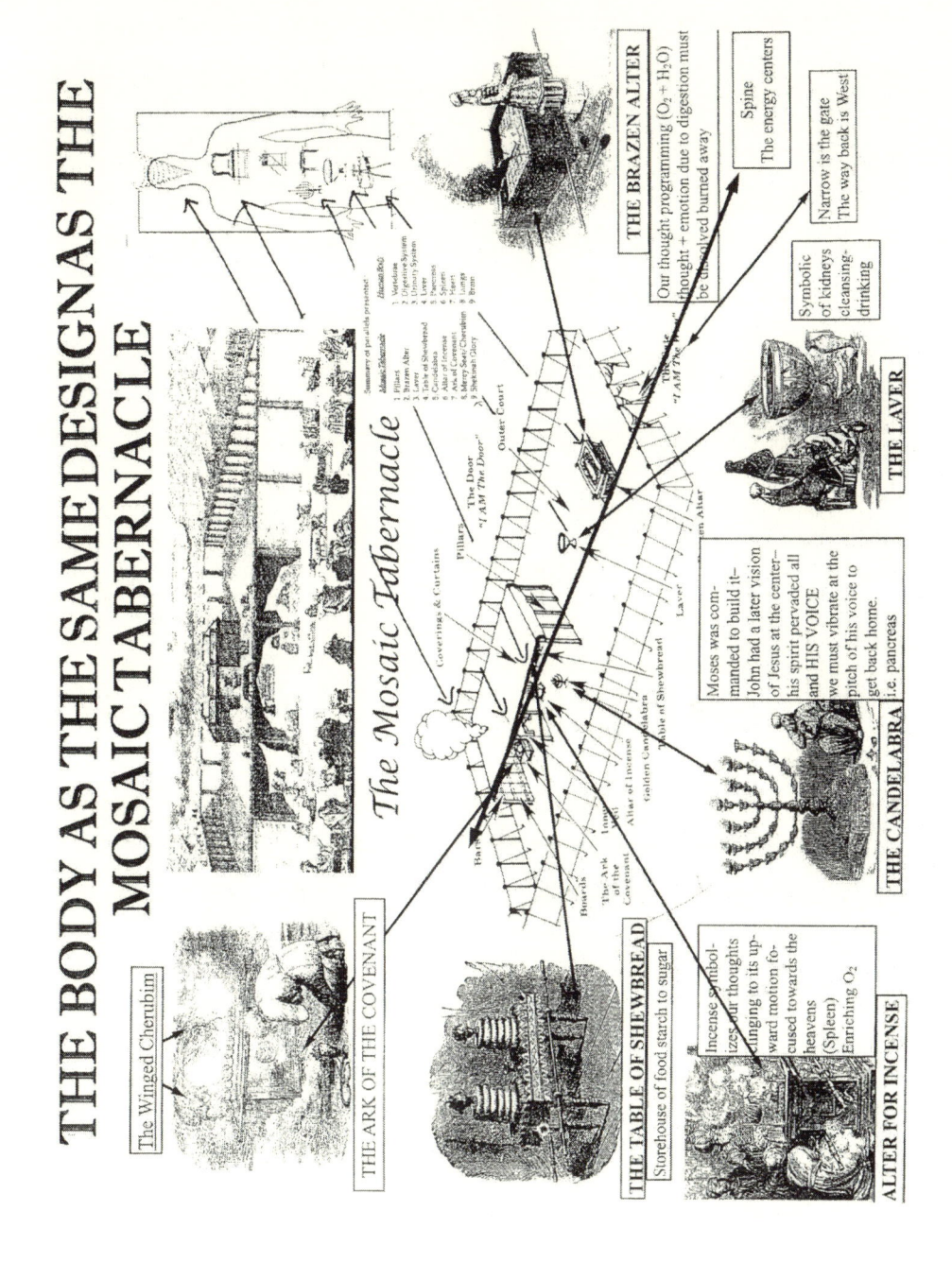

THE BODY AS THE SAME DESIGN AS THE MOSAIC TABERNACLE

The Mosaic Tabernacle

The Winged Cherubim

THE ARK OF THE COVENANT

Summary of parallels presented:
Mosaic Tabernacle — Human Body:
1. Pillars — Ventricles
2. Brazen Altar — Digestive System
3. Laver — Urinary System
4. Table of Shewbread — Pancreas
5. Candelabra — Spleen
6. Altar of Incense — Heart
7. Ark of Covenant — Lungs
8. Mercy Seat Cherubim — Brain
9. Shekinah Glory

Outer Court

The Door "I AM The Door"

Coverings & Curtains

Pillars

Altar of Incense
Golden Candelabra
Table of Shewbread

Boards

The Ark of the Covenant

Inner Altar
Laver
Brazen Altar

"I AM THE"

THE BRAZEN ALTER
Our thought programming ($O_2 + H_2O$) thought + emotion due to digestion must be dissolved burned away

Spine
The energy centers

Narrow is the gate
The way back is West

THE LAVER
Symbolic of kidneys cleansing-drinking

Moses was commanded to build it—John had a later vision of Jesus at the center—his spirit pervaded all and HIS VOICE we must vibrate at the pitch of his voice to get back home.

THE CANDELABRA
i.e. pancreas

THE TABLE OF SHEWBREAD
Storehouse of food starch to sugar

Incense symbolizes our thoughts ringing to its upward motion focused towards the heavens
(Spleen) Enriching O_2

ALTER FOR INCENSE

An Interlude

It was late, but to learn of the *spiritual creation* was so amazing that I could not think of sleep.

Instead, I sat outside the hotel on a stone veranda. There was a full moon and the sounds of the town—dogs barking, children crying, adults in conversation—and then, as time passed, there was a deep, deep silence, as though Mother Mary herself had cast a sacred blanket on all of her pilgrims.

As I sat, the most unexplainable feeling of *joy* permeated my body, a sense of knowing *the true fullness of faith*, a feeling of grand contentment like never before.

The stars emerged brighter than I could have ever imagined, and there was a hint of God hovering near, touching his earthly footstool, the Ark, his dwelling place here in Lalibela, and I fell into a sacred sleep.

The Precious Human Body

"Today is a good day for an authentic Ethiopian coffee," pronounced Brother Benedict. "You certainly have experienced our coffee ceremonies, haven't you?"

I nodded.

We started to walk into the town of Lalibela. Beggars lined the streets, and kids begged for money. Brother Benedict and I smiled at them and kept on walking.

"How did you like last evening with Father K.?"

"Sensational. I'd never heard such things before. The notion that the human body has the design, the architecture, of the Tabernacle of Moses blows my mind, and the idea that the purpose of the human body is to become *spiritually pregnant* with Christ—to be an imitation of Mary—is something so amazing. I feel speechless again."

We had reached the small "bunabet," the coffee shop in town, and we walked in and sat on stools. A woman smiled at us, greeted Brother Benedict, and started to scatter fresh grass on the floor.

"You could further your contemplation of the human body by understanding that its purpose—to be pregnant with Christ—is intimately connected to speech. This is what humans do. *Speak! Hear!* The nature of mankind is to speak and also to hear, and this is of interest since God himself is the *Word*. You are a biologist and teach anatomy, so you can understand that the windpipe carries the air. It winds up the windpipe in the same way that the cloud whirled over the Ark. Knowing this makes one aware that we are to carry the *Word* and only the *Word* with us, to speak only the *Word*, to think only the *Word*, and in that way, we become true Tabernacles—living *temples*."

The woman ground fresh coffee beans for our coffee, and the small room smelled of coffee. She handed us each a bean, this being the custom. Brother Benedict sniffed his and raised his hands with approval.

"Mary provided mankind with the help of God—*the Word in flesh*. The Word becomes incarnate, the one who will speak *the Word*. I have ears to hear it and a mouth to speak it and share it with others. To be pregnant with the *Word* is the highest form of *prayer*. Prayer is the most powerful activity of man, and therefore, we do not pray alone but with *Mary*, because she will help you be transformed by him through the practice of the *Word*. Then his *Word* becomes our word, and his worship becomes ours. We are transformed to another way of life through *his Word* and through being in alignment with it, being pregnant with it. The true purpose of the body is then to be pregnant with Christ and with his Word and to be in constant *adoration* and *prayer.*"

The woman produced the first cups of coffee. We sat in silence reflecting on the day and enjoying the aroma, the fresh grass under our feet, and each sip of the coffee.

The Anointing

It was early evening again, and Father K. was to make his last presentation. The pilgrims gathered early so as not to miss one word.

The sky was again aglow with pinks and purples, and there was a slightly cool breeze when Father K. appeared before the crowd.

"Good evening, brothers and sisters. Welcome! Welcome all pilgrims! This evening, I want to talk to you about the *anointing*. That is, when you live your life in the sacred design, when you live your life like Mary—pregnant with Christ—you will receive the *anointing*, the Presence of God. This is the promise for everyone! Take the time to learn about the Tabernacle and about all of its components—how they help you become like Mary and how they help you to hold *Christ*!

"You will discover amazing things in the process of your study. Aaron's rod, for instance, which was kept inside the Ark, reminds us to expect the miraculous every day. If you do not expect it, what then? Why live in the sacred design if you do not accept all of its benefits?

"Remember that the Tabernacle experience is God's design for approaching him and that *his presence* is what you receive—and *that* can be so powerful that it will influence others. This is our great gift to God—to be filled with his presence, not only for ourselves but for others.

"Let me leave you tonight with the words of Pope John Paul II: *'The body, in fact, and only it, is capable of making visible what is invisible: the spiritual and the divine. It was created to transfer into the visible reality of the world the mystery hidden from eternity in God, and thus to be its sign.'"*

The Blessing

"I cannot believe it is almost time to leave, Brother Benedict. I feel that it will be only after I leave here that I will begin to comprehend Lalibela."

"Come, follow me! This will help you."

We walked down the stone stairway to St. George's Cathedral and entered a special side chapel.

"This is the place where special pilgrims are birthed again," Brother Benedict whispered as he stooped to take off his sandals.

It was cool inside and full of incense. He pointed to the ceiling. There, suspended from the ceiling, were two gold cups. "They are from Solomon's Temple." He then pointed to the floor to a circle lined in gold. "This symbolizes the *Tomb of Adam*. Before your departure, we are giving you a very special blessing, after which you will walk through this door, which is symbolic of Adam's tomb opened, Adam redeemed, Eve redeemed. You reenter the world rebirthed in Christ."

In absolute silence, a priest appeared with a huge gold cross. Brother Benedict guided me into the circle. "Are you ready?"

I nodded.

He took my palms and turned them up and open, ready to receive the anointing with chrism oil.

The priest began to chant a prayer for my rebirth in Christ—a prayer for my protection as I reentered the world in Christ, a prayer for a host of angels to accompany me the rest of my life. The chanting continued while the priest raised the huge cross and blessed my head, my back, my front side, my feet, and my hands. He then anointed my forehead with the oil, bowed, smiled, and disappeared.

Brother Benedict took my hand and led me out the door—the door of the redeemed Eve—and I reentered the world.

"Remember, you are no longer alone now. You do not go through life anymore under your own power, but now you live in his power!"

We walked in silence.

The Manuscript

"To celebrate your special blessing you just received, we do not want you to leave without this most priceless gift," Brother Benedict said in a whisper. "Here is something that might make your going easier. Father K. gave me this for you, because he believes you will be a faithful student. This is a *manuscript* that has many notes for you to read and study. The drawings that Father K. did awhile ago are extremely helpful. Inside is also a booklet that a Father McCarthy from your own country wrote, which is helpful since it is in your native language."

Brother Benedict handed me the manuscript and then gave me a blessing. "My dear Katherine, it has been a great honor to meet you. Take this experience and manuscript home now and share it. Teach it to those who are open to such knowledge, but have discernment; some will just want it for their own use. Protect this knowledge. You carry a *priceless treasure*. Be a true guardian of it. You have taught the nature of the physical creation; now teach the spiritual creation, and the world will be blessed by your life."

We did not say a further word to each other. I turned and walked with sadness as well as great anticipation to the old rusty bus that would take us back to the mountaintop landing area for the flight back to Addis Ababa.

I knew one thing for certain ... that the moment the manuscript was placed in my hands, my life—and life purpose—had changed forever.

And with the manuscript in hand, I recognized that I had experienced *the He Did* event of my life. I had no idea now what would happen in my life, but I knew that it would never be the same—that *Christ* had broken through coming to Lalibela!

Part 3

The I Am

The I Am

Welcome Pilgrim, to the I Am.

You are making good progress.

Do not stop now, but be aware!

The I Am is not one ecstatic event after another, but more often a process whereby the pilgrim is stripped of all that contaminates his or her soul from all that is false and from all that is untrue!

Then the soul can advance!

It anticipates mystical union with God!

The I Am

can be a grueling journey, full of challenges and obstacles, depending on the need

of the soul.

The pilgrim needs to remember, however, that he or she is never alone!

Returning Home

It was a long flight on Air France from Paris to Miami. As the aircraft met the North American continent, there was severe turbulence. Not a sound could be heard from anyone except the hushed sighs and the silent prayers of tense passengers.

The cabin doors finally opened. We had arrived! It was 3:00 p.m. Tired from the long and stressful journey, I followed the passengers, mindful that I would soon step once again on US soil, my homeland, ending a long chapter in my life—that of missionary, wife, and teacher. As I progressed closer to the actual disembarking, I realized, too, that I arrived home as a *widow*, alone and not knowing what was next.

I followed the passengers down the metal ramp. No one spoke, each relieved to be at his or her destination, and then everyone seemed to melt away into the crowd, hiking down the unending airport corridor, pulling out their cell phones and walking faster and faster.

As I proceeded, I was overcome by a strange feeling—a feeling of weakness that was accompanied by a series of disturbing images. I attributed them to my exhaustion, but as I continued, the images became stronger, more like a vision. I saw buildings falling and people in long lines desperate for help. There was a sense of great doom and depression. It startled me.

Afraid that I might be severely sick, I forced myself to continue, hoping to get easily through customs, find a taxi, and make it to my final destination.

Thankfully, I arrived at the customs desk. The agent welcomed me home. The gloomy images dissipated. I found my luggage, got a shuttle, and made it to the hotel.

Showered and relaxed, I studied the Miami skyline. It was very strange to be home, and I was disturbed by the memory of those images.

I thought of my father, an immigrant, who had also served in the US Army. He'd received a special award from President Reagan for his meritorious service in World War II. What would he say? What would his commentary be on the United States today, and more importantly, what advice would he give me as I began to reintegrate into society?

But that was not a possibility. Dad had passed away, and after his death, the family strangely disintegrated, losing all sense of connection and leaving only superficial ties.

I took solace in the realization that, if it had been different, I would not have spent so many years in Ethiopia and perhaps never reached Lalibela—and Lalibela had changed my life forever.

There is nothing that I would exchange for that *one* experience. It was simply the pearl of great price, and it had become the center of my life.

I ordered dinner and sat watching the sunset over Miami, wondering what new adventures awaited me now. By any chance, did those images and visions at the airport earlier hold any special significance? Was it a premonition, a warning, or just plain exhaustion?

Reintegrating

Life had changed. It was no longer like it was in Ethiopia with a house full of young people, full of laughter, people huddled each night around our dinner table. Life *now* had a new rhythm, something like a seesaw—go to work, go shopping, come home, watch TV.

The American workplace appeared different from what I remembered years ago. It was strained, governed by increasing efficiency, obsessed with greed and aggressive advertising, and every effort was made to get me to *consume*!

I sailed from one position to another. Jobs ended—sometimes abruptly—sometimes due to lack of funding, sometimes due to unethical behavior of senior staff, sometimes because of corporate power struggles, and sometimes from the abuse of an impossible workload.

What I experienced by day was echoed on the news at night—cheating politicians, sports idols behaving badly, *megacorporations* stealing private retirement funds, Wall Street bonuses too greedy to comprehend, betrayal after betrayal.

My head spun to keep up with the increasing demand that this society required for one to fully participate.

One Morning in Chemistry Class

And then one morning, as I was in the middle of teaching an honors chemistry class, everything changed. Teachers were requested to turn on the classroom TVs. There it was! There it was for the whole world to see—9/11 in progress!

Suddenly, the images I'd seen at the Miami airport came alive; the living edition of what I had experienced years ago as I arrived home was now playing before my very eyes. Buildings were falling, and there was an instant sense of doom and despair.

Life changed! Americans had become preoccupied. Everything else took a backseat. Life was suddenly an endless replay of the events of 9/11, with endless interpretations and endless predictions for our future as a nation.

I sensed that this was the beginning of a new way of living—that America in that one day had changed forever and that life would never be the same again.

September 11 was the *invitation*, it seemed, to a *new* world—one now besieged with great challenges as well as monstrous natural disasters. I watched in horror as Hurricane Katrina raced toward the Gulf Coast. For weeks, the world observed the unthinkable—people in great need in the United States.

A Distant Memory

By now, Lalibela had become a distant memory. The once so important *manuscript* was filed away in my treasure chest of Ethiopian memories. It seemed to belong to something in my past.

I had returned home, settled into society, accepted my role as an average citizen, and became increasingly consumed by the personal challenges of living everyday life in the United States.

But then there was an *intervention*! By chance, I had accepted an invitation to attend a seminar, "Spirituality In 2008." It was there that I met Sister Paul Emilia, an Adrian Dominican sister.

She talked about *charism*—your personal vocation and purpose in life. The participants then had to share their most amazing moment in life. I talked about Lalibela! Surprisingly, everyone wanted to know more. Sister Paul invited me to speak at St. Joseph Parish.

I answered her with a big yes. It just flew out of my mouth, and in doing so, I knew that something *big* had just happened in my life.

The remainder of the seminar was about the Order of Preachers and the life of St. Dominic and how he knew his purpose. I was so inspired to share the gospel, and it was on that day that I, too, was touched by his fire. I was even more touched by Sister Paul, who, for just a brief while, returned me to that *other place* I'd once experienced—that other world, that place where I once had *touched heaven*—Lalibela.

St. Joseph Parish

Lalibela became a lecture series!

And the lecture series grew into a continuous weekly meeting.

Friday Club was born!

There was a lot of excitement. More and more people participated, and at the same time, I curiously found myself having more and more conversations with Sister Paul about the Dominican life and Dominican spirituality. Just as gently, she whispered, "So why don't you join us as an Adrian Dominican associate?"

As I learned about Dominican spirituality, the four pillars of Dominican life—prayer, study, community, and ministry—and its mission to preach God's love, compassion, and mercy, I found myself infusing my lectures with this *joyous* charism. As a result, Friday Club continued to grow even more.

Space, however, got very tight!

And that is how I met them—the Stillbornes—a very wealthy couple who had heard about Friday Club. They were a handsome couple; they were captivating and full of energy and enthusiasm. Their main interest in life was teaching wellness. They began to attend Friday Club, loved it, and wanted to support its expansion.

Over the next couple of years, Friday Club blossomed, and classes expanded to include Wednesdays and Thursdays. During this time, the Stillbornes were my sole support financially. Their enthusiasm continued, and I trusted them now not only as friends or supporters but like family.

It seemed so fine!

But it even got better. *Way better—unbelievably better*! The Stillbornes purchased a house for me.

With a house, Friday Club could continue, now with its own kitchen and a backyard for all of its classes and celebrations. The best part of it, the very best part of it, was that I would have a permanent home, a place to live the rest of my life.

The Stillbornes found the place and arranged for everything, and I suddenly was living a dream.

It was the talk of the parish! Everyone was amazed! We celebrated for weeks.

But this is what eventually led me to the door of Father Thomas's office.

It was here that the next phase of my life, *the I Am* phase, was placed under his guidance.

Father Thomas

"He is ready for you now."

I nodded.

The receptionist buzzed the door open.

There he stood down the long hallway. "My dear Katherine," he said with his faint Irish brogue. "Come inside, sit here, and make yourself comfortable. I want to hear everything."

"Well, I feel so embarrassed, so very stupid!" I began reaching for a tissue from my purse. "You know how excited I was when the Stillbornes purchased the house two years ago. You were there at the celebration; you blessed the house."

"Oh, I do remember very well. What an event!"

"You remember Black Saturday, last April, when the Stillbornes came by to announce that they were withdrawing the funding for my work? Their explanation was simply that they had other interests now. The next day, I heard that they took off for an extended vacation in Hawaii. I managed to find other sources of funding, and I thought that things would be fine, but no, Father

Thomas. They appeared again on Saturday, October 5—Black Saturday Number Two—a day I will not forget, because this time they came to announce that they were not going to continue to support the house. They would no longer pay the mortgage!"

Father Thomas winced.

I sat silently. Somehow, in telling this tale, I suddenly was confronted with its enormity. It began to take on the shape of a huge mountain.

The Worst Part of It

"I am not even at the worst part of this matter yet, Father. Here is what happened." I started to revisit the sequence of events and facts, counting on my fingers. "Firstly, according to my legal advisor, the Stillbornes managed to finance the house using my credit; there was no disclosure that my sole financial support was totally dependent on their contribution.

"Secondly, the intention at the time of purchase was that the house was to be fully paid for—that was the plan! A home equity line of credit would help finance the materials for seminars and the classes, but at the last minute without my knowing, they decided not to put a penny down and opted for a huge and ridiculous mortgage.

"Thirdly, at the signing, there was champagne, lots of laughter, talk about playing golf, and many papers to sign. After the Stillbornes signed a paper, it was passed to me, and I was directed to sign my name here and here. There was no comment and no warning when the only paper they did *not* sign—the *note* for the house— was silently passed to me for my signature. It made me totally responsible for a $280,000 house. There was no discussion. No one stopped and said, 'Use caution before you sign here; do you know what you are signing?' Of course, I fully trusted them.

"Fourthly, to top it all, they purchased this house from their best friend, who apparently was having difficulty selling it. The list price, the asking price, was never negotiated, and after the signing, a deluxe washer and dryer were taken out of the house and replaced with used machines. There was never an explanation. When I first learned of a mortgage, the Stillbornes explained that it was a faster way to get the house and, 'After all, the total cost of the house is a drop in the bucket, and we are intending to pay it off next month.'

"Fifthly, according to the papers, there was a big profit made with the sale of the house. My legal advisor said to me, 'It seems like someone needed quick cash, and if so, it was at your expense.'

"Sixthly, I never saw the Stillbornes again after that Black Saturday! They just vanished from my life. They simply walked out—no regrets, no remorse, no 'I am sorry you are going to have to move.' Mrs. Stillborne just mumbled under her breath that she was glad they were not going to take the hit for the house. Of course, I did *not* know what that meant at the time."

The End Result

"The end result of this long tale, Father Thomas, is I have been forced into bankruptcy."

He gently pushed his chair back and sat in silence.

"Now, I have legal fees to pay! I have to move out of the house! I have no funds—no funds to move and no funds for legal fees! I have no place to go!"

The Real Facts

Father Thomas looked more pensive. "I think I sense what happened," he said. "Let me ask you, Katherine—just how did these people make their money?"

"They are into wellness products—a meganetwork marketing corporation."

"Katherine, tell me this: what was it about *you* that served them? What was of benefit to them?"

"It was bringing people into a group and providing names and contacts so that they could expand their business. Of course, I was so innocent—so very, very naïve—to think that it *really* was Lalibela that captured their interest. I must say, however, that friends voiced their concerns. They even confronted the Stillbornes directly about making Friday Club a business opportunity.

"The Stillbornes were very convincing! They assured everyone that there was no business interest, and that although they would really not have time to come, they just wanted to promote spirituality, because that was part of wellness. However, I found it curious that they *never* attended the seminars and classes. I sent them handouts and reports of what happened at each class, but never did I get a response. I always assumed that they were so busy, and later, I began to wonder if I was a mere tax write-off. But they had easy access to the names of all of the participants of Friday Club, and most were contacted in various ways by their business associates in an effort to expand *their* wellness business. So, yes, that was the big benefit—names, addresses, and contacts—and many of the participants of Friday Club resented the intrusion."

When People Are Used

"I was so blind. I was so naïve, so trusting, Father Thomas. What am I going to do? But now, of course, I *see*! When my work was not providing enough new contacts for their business, they lost interest. They wanted just to ditch the project, ditch me, and ditch the house. I think it is as simple as that, Father Thomas."

"My dear Katherine, it is an experience you will *not* forget. It is an event of great betrayal. What they did was morally wrong, but it is one of the most important lessons we can learn on this earth. When we do charity for the sake of our *own* interests, it brings devastation! When we *use* people to satisfy our own needs and ends, it is a great sin. It is a result of being aligned with darkness."

"But these Stillbornes constantly talked about Jesus and spirituality!"

"Then I have to say that they might be imposters—what we could call 'Christian atheists.' They do not understand the basic precepts of the faith. They needed to persuade you that they had a moral conscience and that they were really interested in your well-being. They did that and gained your trust. One must be on watch, on constant vigil, to discern the foundation from which a person is operating. Unless you build everything on the truth, nothing will stand; nothing will last, and nothing will promote peace or joy. The Stillbornes' charity was one of self-interest. This is why you do not belong in that house or with them, and it is ultimately why you are being released from it all. It is part of your *I Am* experience—to be washed of all that is *not true*! Consider yourself rescued!"

He continued, "It hurts! It is painful! It is a lonely experience to be taken as a widow! But being angry at them really does not help. You are called to find *forgiveness*. Think of it this way—we cannot get angry at people for who they *really* are! Their name is curious, I must say—Stillborne. It is said that all humanity is stillborn into the world, and then by the grace of God, some find Christ and are born into *everlasting life*." Father Thomas smiled. "We only can pray for their conversion before they hurt too many people. What you have faced is a microcosm of what is happening in this nation. The *using* of people for financial gain breeds greed, arrogance, and then devastation. It happens when people have forgotten *God* or when people do not know *God* at all. I think the *real* test is that they would not come here to my office to facilitate *reconciliation*. They refused. So now you must reconcile this here with me so that you can go on with your life."

A Hidden Wisdom

"But how do I react and respond to the Stillbornes now? I still feel the urge to scream and to throw tomatoes." Katherine laughed. "They just walked away. They would not come here to talk it out."

"Let me share this with you, Katherine," replied Father Thomas. "Sadly, most people learn a little about Christian dogma and doctrine and think, 'That is it—I understand the Christian experience.' Doctrine is an invitation to that which is greater—the mystery of Christ. Even those who are well versed in scripture are often ignorant of the deeper, most awesome power of Christianity. Deep in between the neurons of each body lurks darkness and inherent evil. It is part of our very fallen nature. If we fully comprehend this, it is easy to understand that evil finds its way into groups, organizations, institutions, governments, or millionaires like the Stillbornes. Evil is sick and can be ugly. You are seeing it firsthand in this experience.

"The great *secret* to fighting evil, to making right what the Stillbornes have done, mysteriously does *not* require a superstrong person. It does not require a sword, a quick mouth, or even an attorney. Certainly, we do not want to throw tomatoes." Father Thomas chuckled. "To fight evil just requires you to work with Christ. That is a hidden secret, a great wisdom. And we even have a perfect model to follow! The Blessed Mother teaches us how to work with Christ. She stood silently at the foot of the cross. I am sure it was difficult to do that. I am sure that she cried, wept, and maybe she wanted to scream or throw tomatoes. Nevertheless, *she remained silent*. She *knew* what was going to happen. She knew the end of the story, and so do you. That is what is so amazing. As a *Christian*, you already know the end of this story with the Stillbornes. So we follow her example! Stand at the foot of this cross, but be *silent* like Mary!

"In doing so—like Mary—you unite yourself with the light of Christ. Just stand in *his light*, in his presence, and in his Word. This is enough to transform evil into the *light*.

"Of course, if you share this advice with people outside, they will insist that you've lost your mind. They will encourage you to get an attorney and to get tough. But keep in mind that this is the enormity of *Christianity*. It will work like this; first, the darkness of this situation will be drawn out and *exposed*. All you do is carry on with your daily activities. Do what you have to do to get through the processes. Trust, have faith, and you will be carried through in a way you cannot imagine!

"And remember as a rule that *evil* and darkness are usually most successfully exposed through the most vulnerable of persons like you, a *widow*. You appear weak and small in the eyes of the Stillbornes. They might think they fooled you, but the great secret is that you will fool them in your silence and in being united to *Christ*.

It is then you become most powerful! Perhaps, it was your role to be a victim soul—to be that which started to draw out the evil into the light. But you cannot correct this, because no matter what you say to the Stillbornes, it will not be heard; you cannot correct their thinking. You cannot do this on your own. This could be a test of your greater faith. Now let Christ intervene and trust that he alone knows how to respond to evil and to the darkness. As the darkness is drawn out, the *light* of Christ transforms it. The secret is to be totally consecrated to *him* and to be obedient to *him*.

"Have confidence that Mary is with you and that she protects you through this, and read the parables and the teachings of Jesus. See how this secret teaching is there hidden for the few who are really seeking *the truth of Christ*. Now apply this mystery to how you respond to the Stillbornes and wait and *see*. I promise you that you will be amazed! The Stillbornes give you the opportunity now to practice your faith at a totally new level—on the level of the *I Am*."

A Miracle Priest

It was my next visit.

"I am so glad to see you again!" Father Thomas said. "Sit and tell me what is going on. How are you doing?"

"Well, I am starting the legal process. I am fully responsible for this house, Father Thomas. I still cannot believe that these people did this to me—a veteran, a missionary, a widow. Even if I get out from under this, I will never again be able to have the possibility of purchasing a house, a condo, or a car."

Tears just ran down my cheeks. Father Thomas offered tissues. I felt powerless. I wondered what my future would be.

"Listen to me," said Father Thomas. "There is a big gift in this, and I already see the *miracle*, as well." He smiled. "Be patient. I sense that in Ethiopia, in this place called Lalibela, you had an experience of great immensity. You experienced the light, and it ultimately led you to the *truth*, to the Universal Church. To teach about *light* and to teach about Christ, it is also helpful to understand *darkness* and what it is like, how it presents itself in the world, and how to encounter it. This experience, this challenge, prepares you to really relate to those who are going through similar situations. Suffering through trials always brings a gift! Once the gift is received, I must say that I have seen my share of *miracles*.

"Pray and trust *him* that a great plan is unfolding *perfectly* through you. Do not condemn the abusers; they are who they are. Try to find forgiveness for them by praying for their true conversion."

The Chalice of the Silver Maple

"How was your Easter?" Father Thomas inquired.

I was back in his office. "I had to come to tell you," I began, "that during your Easter service, I started to feel these words emerge in my head. It is a series of questions, each of which I had to answer. I wrote them down for you. Before I begin, you realize that the words *Silver Maple* are from the address of my house; it is on Silver Maple Way, and so this is what I heard."

I began to read.

"Do you love me?" Christ whispered.

"Yes, *of course," I replied.*

"Then drink my Chalice of the Silver Maple. Do you love me enough for me to take away your financial support?"

"Oh, Lord. What will I do then? Well, if you must, okay, **yes,** *" I replied.*

"Do you love me enough to take your home?"

"Oh, Lord, why? Really? Must you? Where shall I go, Lord? Okay, if it is your will, Lord, **yes**," I replied.

"Do you love me enough that I leave you abandoned?"

"Oh, Lord, really? Okay, **yes,** if it is your will, Lord," I replied.

"Do you love me enough to leave you penniless?"

"Well, Lord, okay!" For now my eyes were beginning to see. "Yes, Lord!"

"Do you love me enough to go to trial and to stand amongst lawyers?"

"**Yes**, of course, Lord, because the more you are taking away, the more I see that there is only you, and amazingly, I am starting to feel peace and even joy!"

"You have now drunk the Chalice of the Silver Maple, and in doing so, I will rescue you from the world of profanity, greed, arrogance, self-interest, and false charity, from a world that can only offer you nothing, from a world that promises you everything but can only bring you ruin and death."

I paused, waiting for Father Thomas to comment.

He smiled. "It is a great Easter present. I believe you have surrendered the *Silver Maple event* to Christ. It is a remarkable breakthrough on your spiritual journey through the *I Am*. In releasing the house, you release this false charity, this false relationship, and you become—in a way—purified. It appears that Christ is near. He is ready to heal you of this betrayal. Stay near *him* now. Be thankful for this. It is truly remarkable. Be ready for your life to quickly change. The key event for the *I Am* state is to surrender all to Christ. You have surrendered your income, your home, and your possessions to *him*. Now wait and see what *he* does to replace what you think you lost." He chuckled.

Resurrection of the Manuscript

Daily life was now a routine of constant sorting, packing boxes, and discarding of possessions. I had to move. The house was in the process of foreclosure. I had no other option than to declare a bankruptcy. Tears filled my eyes each day as I walked through the house on Silver Maple, surrendering to the unknown.

The project was emotionally embellished by the fact that I had no idea where I was going. Did I need to downsize to a one-bedroom dwelling? Did I need to downsize to an efficiency? Did I need to plan for all of my belongings to be kept in permanent storage? Would I end up in my Jeep?

The phone rang. It was Sister Paul Emilia. She said, "I am checking in on you. How are you doing, and do you need our help? We were talking about you last night and wanted to know if you're practicing everything you *teach*." She laughed. "Have you asked for the *miracle* yet? Maybe you need to reread that manuscript you have, Teacher!"

We talked and laughed, and as soon as I hung up, I went to find *the manuscript*.

I unpacked my already packed Ethiopian chest. There it was—*the manuscript* that Brother Benedict had so graciously given me upon my departure from Lalibela.

There was a copy of the final blessing, too. "You will be sent *angels.*" Suddenly, I realized that Sister Paul Emilia and the Adrian Dominicans were the angels promised to me, and so I took their message seriously.

I did not pack one more thing. I sat on the couch and spent the night rereading it.

How could I have forgotten it? How could I have let this *spiritual treasure* sit so long in the chest? I had mentioned the manuscript in my lectures, but I'd never restudied it since returning home.

Rereading the Manuscript

It was late.

The *manuscript*, that document given to me by Brother Benedict in Lalibella, reveals the Tabernacle Experience, the twelve keys to receiving the *anointing*. It now was out of storage, sitting on my lap.

I opened it, began to read, and could not stop.

> The power of this *manuscript* is that each of the parts of the Tabernacle, each of the components, reveals a hidden wisdom, a spiritual practice that ultimately ushers the pilgrim into the Holy of Holies, the place of the Shekinah, the Presence of God. The pilgrim needs only to follow each step.
>
> #1. *The gate* of the Tabernacle is like a door. It symbolizes the *Way*. It is the invitation to *know Jesus*.
>
> #2. *The brazen altar* is the total consecration to Jesus. We give him all. We sacrifice all for *him*.
>
> #3. *The laver* symbolizes the Blood of the Lamb. It symbolizes forgiveness for our sins, the Sacrament of Reconciliation.

#4. *The Golden Lampstand* represents the *truth*. It represents the revelation of knowledge. Here, we pray for God to enlighten our understanding so that we can progress to the Holy of Holies.

#5. *The Table of Shewbread* symbolizes the Eucharist. This is the food for spiritual pregnancy. This is what nourishes you and sustains you through the spiritual pilgrimage of life.

#6. *The altar of incense* represents praise and worship. Here, we forget ourselves, we concentrate on our Lord, and we begin to flow like incense out of ourselves.

#7. *The veil* of the Tabernacle represents the entrance into the Holy of Holies. The veil represents the body broken in death, Christ on the cross. The pilgrim now dies to self as Christ did on the cross, and in doing so, the pilgrim receives the anointing—this grace that loves, heals, and serves. Accepting this *cross*, we become obedient to *him*. The cross is linked to the *anointing*.

It is here I stopped.

I realized that because I knelt before Christ—because I consecrated myself to him and read the Word daily and listened to it—it made it possible for me to embrace my cross. I was able to surrender the house, the income, and the betrayal of the house contract with a certain sense of joy and forgiveness.

I partake daily of praise and worship, symbolized by the incense, the food for spiritual pregnancy, and the Eucharist. And just now in my life did I embrace my *cross*. I surrendered the house, the income, and the betrayal of the house contract all to *him*.

I had drunk from the cup, *the Chalice of the Silver Maple,* and I was now free to proceed to the next step.

> #8. The flow of the covenant is necessary to experience the outflowing of God—to receive his love, his grace, to let him be my God, my source, and to be fully in covenant with him.

> #9. *The cherubim* above the Ark lets us enter into silence and awe, to walk in the power of his presence, letting your whole being grow still.

> #10. *Aaron's rod* represents the miraculous, because it was the rod of Aaron that miraculously budded. It therefore became symbolic of the supernatural flow of God's wisdom, love, and power. It is here that, having practiced all of the keys to the anointing, we start to expect the miraculous. It is here that we realize that God wants to give us infinitely more than anything we can dare to hope for. It is here that we can be brought into total dependency on the supernatural gifts, miracles, and healings.

It is here that I again paused.

Oh, my goodness, I had practiced so much of the Tabernacle experience even during these difficult times, but I had not once stopped to *expect the miracle*.

I was suddenly burning with hope.

I read on.

> #11. The *Golden Pot of Manna* relates to our daily supply of sustenance. As the pilgrim remains devoted to this path, God provides a river of blessings; he will supply us with all of our needs.
>
> #12. The *Ark of the Covenant* is the footstool of God. Here, God meets us; here is the Shekinah, the Presence, here the pilgrim receives the *anointing*, the grace, the overflowing of blessings, the miracles, *and his timing is perfect*.

I fell silent.

Here was the key—the secret of getting out of Silver Maple—putting this event of betrayal behind me.

I fell on my knees and asked Mary for help.

I need the *anointing*. I *need to expect the miracle*.

The Next Day

The next morning, I dutifully resumed my arduous task of sorting, discarding, and packing when the phone rang.

It was Bailey Roe.

She lived on a farm way south of the house on Silver Maple. All I knew about Bailey was that she lived simply, thought of the needs of others all of the time, and took care of stray pets and children.

She wanted to know if she could come to the house on Silver Maple for a short visit. She had some Christmas presents to deliver.

She came.

We talked.

She was stunned by my predicament.

Bailey got up from the table and started to walk around the house.

I followed her as she walked around looking at the ceilings and walls and opening up cabinets as though for inspection.

"Would you ever want to stay here?" she inquired.

"Well, I poured all of my meager savings into the garden to make it a real sanctuary for all those who came here, but it is not a question of what I want. I must leave. The house is headed for foreclosure."

"But if you could keep it, would you want it?" Bailey asked.

"Well, I thought I would live here forever—that this was it. That is why I poured my heart and soul into it, but it is out of the question now. I have to look to the reality of my situation. I have to pack up and be ready at any minute to go."

"You are not answering my question! Would you like to stay here?" she asked again.

"I never really thought about it. This happened so suddenly. In days, I found myself in a lawyer's office learning about the betrayal of the house contract. After that, I have just concentrated on what is next and on what I am going to do. I suppose, however, that the house on Silver Maple has become a symbol of betrayal."

"I thought so. I just wanted to make sure," she said. "I could arrange to buy it, but I think you are finished with this place."

I stood silent. I could not believe what I had just heard.

The Mystical Bailey Roe

Bailey defied description. She appeared ageless, uncomplicated, and yet mysterious.

I first met Bailey shortly after I came home from Africa. There was an advertisement in the paper for pet lovebirds. It was time to have a new pet. Down to Bailey's farm I went. I came home with the sweetest lovebird and a new friend, Bailey Roe. We kept in contact.

Like a real Santa Claus, Bailey would appear almost unannounced, delivering her holiday splendor. Out of her truck would come endless wrapped goodies—all practical items that, in one way or another, became some of my most useful items. Curiously, I noticed that the items she gave were the most useful during that particular year—hurricane items during a year when we had three and sweaters during a year of extreme cold. How did she know?

And so the years passed, and Bailey was always there in the background as the subject of discussion and wonder. Just how did she know what I needed? She became a subject of conversation with my friends. They would inquire, "How is your personal Santa?"

But nothing prepared me for this afternoon when Bailey said that it was time for her to go.

She took care of so many kids—some relatives, some not—and countless animals. Now she had to get back to the farm, but on the way out, she stopped, turned to me, and said, "Go look for a condo that you like and give me a call!"

I stood speechless as she got in her truck.

She started to back out of the driveway. She slowed down, rolled down the window, and said, "So go look and call me, and I will take care of the rest!"

The Miracle

"Father Thomas, I cannot wait to tell you what has happened!"

He stretched out his hands, leading me into his office. As I sat before him, I had the strange feeling that he already *knew* the surprise I was about to reveal.

"I have to start at the very beginning," I announced.

Father Thomas just grinned. "Take your time."

"A miracle has happened. A week ago, a friend purchased a condo for me to live in."

"Oh, my goodness," answered Father Thomas with a big grin.

"Not only that—she purchased it without even seeing it. She just wrote out a check, and it was done. That is not all, Father Thomas. You will not believe it. She put in a new air-conditioning unit, a new hot water heater, put up storm shutters, purchased a new door, a washer and dryer, and had the electrician come up and fix everything. She paid for my move and helped me with many extras."

"Who is she?" Father Thomas asked.

"Her name is Bailey Roe."

"How did you ever get to know such a saint?"

"Let me begin by saying that we had a celebration at the new residence last weekend. Bailey came. Joanna, my friend, took pictures. She took pictures of everyone there—Bev, Sharon, Louise, Peggy, and Janet, and she took pictures of my St. Mary statue and pictures of Bailey, too! The next week, Joanna called me. 'This is so odd. I am sorry,' she said. 'Everyone's picture turned out great, but there is no picture of St. Mary and no picture of Bailey.'

"We were silent for a few seconds. We both knew what the other was thinking.

"'Remember St. Francis?' I said to Joanna. 'Oh, yes,' she replied.

"During our celebration, Bailey disappeared for awhile, but she returned to the door carrying the most beautiful statue of St. Francis. 'This is for you,' she said, quietly holding the statue. 'Where would you like it?'

"Everyone admired it as Bailey kept holding it effortlessly. My friends took their time before deciding that it should be placed on the end table under the palm.

"It was not until the following day that I went to pick up the statue. I could not. It would not budge. It was solid concrete.

"I wondered, 'How did she carry this from the parking lot up the stairs and continue to hold it until we finally decided to put it here on this table?'"

Father Thomas sat back in his chair. He smiled.

"What else can I say? Who would believe me, anyway? All I know is that Bailey takes care of stray pets, homeless kids, and lives as simply as a saint.

"It was one thing to have a place to sleep, a place that felt safe, but it was something else to experience the generosity of a new air conditioner, heater, door, and so on.

"It made me fall silent; it still does. It will forever."

You Knew This Would Happen

"I can tell that you knew this would happen, Father Thomas. You knew that there would be a miracle."

"Well, we can always pray for one," he answered.

"Ever since I came to your office and you have been my spiritual guide through this Silver Maple event, I noticed something very strange. It's like this—my friend Joanna told me that, on the Feast Day of Guadalupe, she prayed that Mary would be the guide to get me through this process. Since then, every key event has taken place on a church feast day. On Christmas, a bankruptcy lawyer called me and offered his services. On the Feast Day of the Baptism of the Lord, there was the court hearing for the bankruptcy. It was over in minutes without complication. On the Feast Day of the Presentation of Our Lord, I received notice from the court that I had complied with all requirements. On the Feast Day of the Annunciation of Our Lord, I received the final decree releasing me from any further legal or financial responsibility. On Easter Sunday, I received the Chalice of the Silver Maple, the gift in all of this. On the Feast Day of the Nativity of John the Baptist, I received a donation to pay the remaining legal fees. And now, on the Feast Day of the Transfiguration of Our Lord, Bailey Roe purchased the condo."

"This is what it is like to live *in the inside*—to live in the kingdom on Earth, the church. This is what you could call the Tabernacle experience," began Father Thomas. "Your friend Joanna did the right thing. She entrusted this process to the Blessed Mother. All she needs is to be asked, and so what you have experienced is what so many long for and do not know that it is *at hand*. It is available to them all. All you have to do is go *inside*. It is available to all that enter into *the I Am*. But now tell me more about this mysterious miracle woman. I am most interested to get to know her."

A Final Reflection

"So now, Father Thomas, what do you think those images—those visions—were at the Miami airport?"

"Well, it could have certainly been a warning that a *fall* of some sort was imminent. This country had been so blessed. It has been the hope of the world, but it forgot the foundation on which it stood. Its source was God, but it has clearly forgotten. The images could have been a warning of your own imminent fall. This was to become your *cross*. I think you came home in a way, innocent as a lamb. As a widow, you were easy prey for the wolf. The amazing thing is that you recognized that this would be your *cross*. Your Lalibela experience helped you to understand what was going on, to embrace the cross, not run away but to surrender to it. That was the *key*, because once you do that—once you surrender to what is—Christ is there. His power is greater than yours and for sure greater than that of any wolf!

"The Tabernacle experience is a metaphor for the spiritual journey on earth. You make the decision to enter the Tabernacle, and then we work through the challenges of the outer court and finally enter into *inner court*. Here is the sweetness. Here are the miracles."

"So what is the lesson that I should take from this?" I asked.

"Beware of the Christian atheist! They are now prolific. It is an epidemic! Unless a person is rooted in *Caritas in Veritate*—Charity in Truth—*run*! Run away fast!" Father Thomas laughed. "You understand what I mean? Keep your vigil lamp on."

Part 4

Living in the I Am

Dear Pilgrim, you have come so far.

You have passed through the I Am Not,

you received the He Did,

and you have encountered the I Am.

Now you continue the journey deeper and deeper

into the depths of the I Am experience.

Keep forging ahead, Pilgrim, until you

sense the mystical marriage at hand,

the Divine Union.

For it is here that you join the saints!

A Time for Celebration

"You need revitalization, renewal, reenergizing!" Joanna announced.

"You are right, but how do I do that?" I replied.

The Chalice of the Silver Maple event was an agonizing and prolonged affair, and it took its toll. I felt beaten, older, hammered, embarrassed, so naïve, and so used. It seemed that my energy would disappear the moment I reflected on the enormity of the betrayal. It was still too much to fully grasp.

"So what about it?" Joanna was working her magic. She is that rare soul on the planet, the one who can sense the miracle at hand, the one who is able to lift others out of the density of their own experience. She navigates through life not totally part of the material world but rather hovering somewhere between earth and heaven. She has been my faithful companion, and I learned to *really* listen to her.

However, I was also aware that there were those who could not comprehend her continual *joy*, her ability to see the outcome even when things are so very dark. I was thankful that I could appreciate her rareness, the gift she brought to me. She constantly advised me, "Look up, look up! Focus on the miracle that is about to happen!" What I learned was to listen to this amazing soul!

And so here was another example of Joanna urging me up out of my density to envision a miracle. "Joanna, I am bankrupt. I cannot go anywhere!"

"Pray to Mary and ask her to guide you to a retreat!"

I did.

The next thing I knew, a ticket was at my door.

Printed on the envelope was, *"To travel to Medjugorje as a pilgrim is to travel to the edge of heaven."*

I could not believe my eyes. It was a ticket for Bosnia and Herzegovina. I was going to Medjugorje, the edge of heaven.

I jumped for *joy*. I jumped with amazement and disbelief! I wondered, "How is this possible? Who sent this? I have to find suitcases, and oh, I wonder what the weather is like there now?"

The Nature of the Pilgrim

There was more. Inside the envelope, I found a note.

Welcome, Dear Pilgrim,

Here are some facts that you should know about a pilgrimage!

In the purest sense, think of your upcoming pilgrimage as a reenactment of the earthly soul's journey through time and space, through the trials of this world and the journey to the promised land.

Your body is required to go on a pilgrimage. In fact, every true, well-designed pilgrimage starts with the body. The long journey to the destination exhausts the body. It is supposed to. A tired body does not have the energy to think a lot. Therefore, the mind slowly is turned off. The soul can now emerge and hear the *Word of God*.

A pilgrimage is an exodus. It is leaving behind that which has consumed us. We need to journey to a strange land to quiet the mind. It cannot run on habitual programs. The soul is now able to communicate more easily with the divine—messages are received, and pilgrims can be changed.

So today, dear pilgrim, have your intentions for this journey written out. Do not leave without them.

It only took me three seconds before my intentions were clear. I wanted to find true forgiveness for the Stillbornes, and I wanted to know what was next in my life—what God was calling me to do.

The ability to find *authentic forgiveness* is the very key to our health. We cannot heal a body that has a wounded soul. I knew for my well-being that I had to forgive so that a new life could begin.

And though the Stillbornes refused *reconciliation*, I had to find my own without them. I had to *find the real gift* of the Silver Maple event so that I could really come and see the Stillbornes as agents used for my spiritual transformation. Once we can raise tragic events to this level, forgiveness pours out like water.

Medjugorje

And so there I was at *the edge of heaven*, the most serene, beautiful village, far away from the cares of the profane world and from the events of the past year. Here I was in a paradise, a place of *Mary*—a village with no TVs, no newspapers, no blaring music, but rather the sound of an unending rosary, of pilgrims praying their way up Apparition Hill, where Mary appeared so many years ago to a group of young children.

And so it was that when I reached the top of Apparition Hill, I could hear her, too. I could hear Mary whispering these unbelievable, amazing words:

"You are at the edge of heaven, child. You have arrived! Medjugorje is the living communal experience of the sacred design, an experience of a true community of people choosing to live in the inside the Tabernacle—living in holiness, living in vigil.

"Medjugorje is my gift to the world so that they can experience heaven and to be on the edge of it.

"You have been rescued from the culture of corruption. I sent my angels to rescue you. Now please make it your life mission to teach about the spiritual journey—the I Am Not, the He Did, and the I

Am. Teach about Lalibela, the Tabernacle, the living Tabernacle, and the precious human body.

"You have taught about the physical creation of the body. Now teach the spiritual creation of the body."

Reentry Back into the World

As I returned home, I realized the *bitter sweetness* of the pilgrim—the inevitability of returning to the physical world and all of its complications. This time, the difference is that my *vigil light was on*, and I was no longer naïve. I was fully aware that I was back in the profane world, full of darkness, trickery, and falsehood.

I was now armed with wisdom found in Alexander de Rouville's *The Imitation of Mary*. *"Guard the treasure you have been given. A single inopportune occasion is enough to destroy you. One day does not guarantee the next. Be forced to live in continual watchfulness, and bear in mind that never yet have you had dealings with the world without being worse off in God's eyes that when you began."*

I was certain of one thing—that I was to teach about the spiritual journey and Lalibela and to help people articulate their own *He Did* experience. I was to teach the invitation of the bridegroom to the inner court, the sancta sanctorum, the place of divine intimacy, the sacred romance. This is what every soul yearns for.

As I would now embark on sharing my own story, so I would also be able to share how I found ways to heal deep betrayal. I realized that had it not been for Lalibela, I could not articulate the process of the spiritual journey. If it had not been for the Stillbornes, I would not have been brought to my knees. I would not have encountered Christ and learned that it is ultimately the Christ we need. I would not have experienced that he provides better and more abundantly than we could ever imagine for ourselves. I now could share about the nature of false charity and how it always leads to destruction, chaos, sadness, and hurt. I would be able to teach about Charity in Truth—that it is the remedy to every hurt in the world and the remedy for suffering.

If it were not for the Chalice of the Silver Maple, I would not be able to share the experience of Bailey Roe, an incarnation of the Good Samaritan, who not only picks up the thrown away, discarded soul, but provides lavishly for her. It is a story that inspires. To have had a personal experience of *the Good Samaritan* is awesome and needs to be shared, because it gives *hope to all*.

And so it was in the sharing of these experiences that I realized one day that I had reached my heart's desire. I found absolute *joy*, I was able *to touch heaven*, and now I wanted to teach it.

Teaching *To Touch Heaven*

"Our *I Am Not* events of life are really not so varied. Basically, they are about ways in which we attempted to find *eros*. Instead of having our eye on finding true eros, we settle for a pseudo, false eros," I began.

It was a warm spring day in Palm Beach as I started a seminar for the Women of Faith Conference. It had been a long road for me—the journey through the *I Am Not* to the *He Did* and now through the *I Am*.

The amazing blessing I had received in Lalibela with Brother Benedict had indeed worked. It had kept me protected and also provided me with angels.

The Dominican Sisters had embraced me in their community as an associate, taught me about St. Dominic, and helped me take on the role of a kind of preacher. It was in their presence that I could strangely feel that Lalibela Moment again. I could recapture it. This was such a help to me during the more challenging times. The Dominicans were truly the angels promised in the blessing so long ago. Without them, I would have not survived the storms.

"Who would believe this story?" I mused as I looked out on the participants. The once teacher of the physical sciences, the once US Army captain, the once missionary, was now teaching the spiritual creation to an audience where almost every seat was taken.

It was time to refocus, and so I continued, "As we pursue pseudo eros, there is one outcome—frustration, dissatisfaction, sometimes depression, anxiety, and despair. It is the *He Did* experience of our lives that offers us the *great* invitation to the discovery of *true eros*, which is the key to divine intimacy. Everyone has had a *He Did moment*. Most people have stored it away. They did not know what to do with it, and so it remains in storage. The good news is that we can retrieve it! It is not totally lost. Finding it is like the discovery of a true spiritual medicine. It can reenergize us, heal us, and motivate us!

"The *He Did* event of our lives is like a cryptogram that we need to study, for in doing so, it reveals everything about our lives. For example, my *He Did* moment occurred in seeing a cathedral. But what can be so important about seeing a cathedral, one could ask? A cathedral can be described as *the true home of the soul*. And if we had the time to review all of the major events in my life, you could clearly see that they have revolved around finding a *true home*. Hence, my *He Did* moment in Lalibela was an invitation to explore the essence of the cathedral—to plunge into the cathedral as a cryptogram—and that is ultimately what I did. I found that the design of the cathedral is related to the design of the Tabernacle and that the design of the Tabernacle reveals the spiritual creation of the human body. Do you see how this works? The cathedral opened up a new world for me.

"You can see that my *He Did* moment changed everything in my life. It literally took over my life! It became a new vocation for me; it brought me into different relationships, into a different place in life, into a new lifestyle, and into a new community. And the same is true for *your He Did* moment. It reveals so much. Once you discern what it is, the *He Did* moment can reveal your program for happiness. It can reveal your greatest desire, your purpose on earth, your calling. Your *He Did* moment can renew and reenergize your life, relationships, and family life.

"In working privately with individuals, the uncovering of the *He Did* moment is a very exciting moment. Many times, I hear people gasp at what they discover. They are astonished and amazed. Many ask how they could have not seen it before; it quickly becomes obvious to them.

"The *He Did* event can also be translated into artwork. It can be fashioned into a personal icon, a coat of arms. We can use personal icons to energize us, reminding us of that which is important, helping us to make decisions in alignment with our very spiritual journey, which helps us reach the *I Am* state with greater ease. To translate your *He Did* moment into art is to have a portrait and *image of your very soul*.

"So, are you ready to discover the *He Did* moment in your life?"

For More Information

For copies of the companion workbook, copies of the manuscript, seminar schedules, and private sessions, visit our website.

Manufactured By: RR Donnelley
                   Momence, IL USA
                   February, 2011